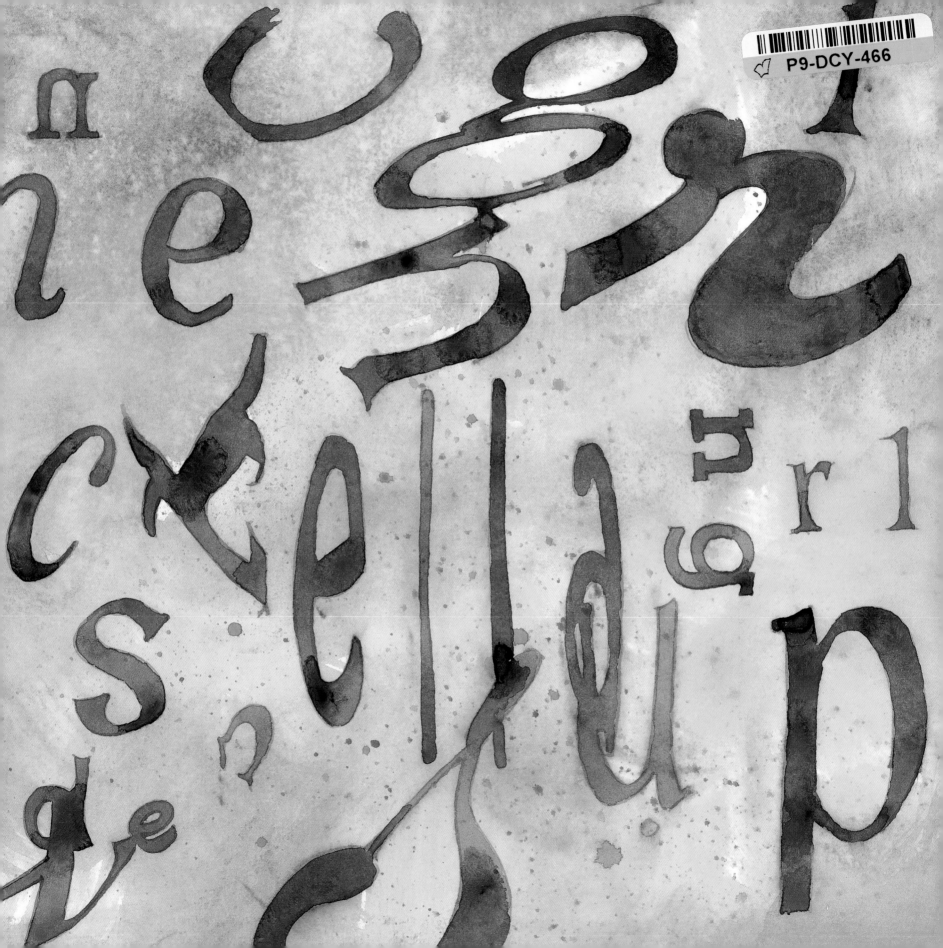

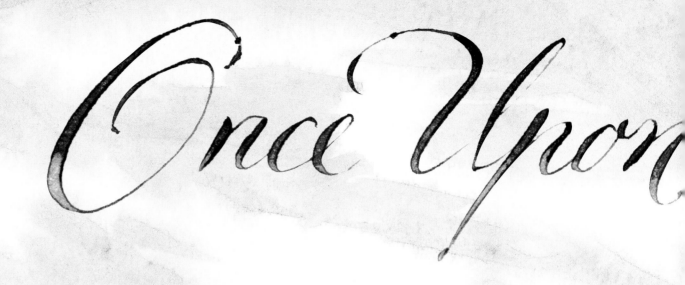

For my dear friend Ann —with love from Niki

Hand-lettering by Andrew van der Merwe
First published in Great Britain by Frances Lincoln Limited, 2003
Printed and bound in Singapore
First American edition, 2003
1 3 5 7 9 10 8 6 4 2

Library of Congress Cataloging-in-Publication Data
Daly, Niki.
     Once upon a time / story and pictures by Niki Daly.— 1st American ed.
       p.   cm.
     Summary: Sarie struggles when she reads aloud in class in her South African school, but then
she and her friend Auntie Anna find a book about Cinderella in Auntie Anna's old car and begin
to read together.
     ISBN 0-374-35633-5
     [1. Reading—Fiction.   2. Friendship—Fiction.   3. Schools—Fiction.   4. Blacks—South
Africa—Fiction.   5. South Africa—Fiction.]   I. Title.

PZ7.D1715 On 2003
[E]—dc21
                                                                                        2002024516

a Time

Story & Pictures by

Niki Daly

FARRAR, STRAUS AND GIROUX • NEW YORK

By eight o'clock the Little Karoo was starting to bake, sending the scent of wild herbs into the dry air. The dirt road to Hopefield, straight as a ruler, stretched forever. Sarie knew the road well. She walked along it every day to school and back again. The long walk did not bother her—she was a dreamer and her legs were strong. It was school that bothered her.

When Mr. Adonis said, "Children, take out your reading books," a sick feeling would grip Sarie, making her hands tremble and her voice disappear.

Sarie hated reading aloud in class.

Those words! So many of them—running together, row after row, page after page. They tripped up her tongue. She stuttered and stammered over them. When it was her turn to read, the children behind her giggled.

"Take your time, Sarie," Mr. Adonis said kindly.

"Take your time, Sarie!" teased Charmaine and Carmen after school.

"Take your time!" joined in the smaller children.

Only Emile stood back and said nothing. He knew that Charmaine and Carmen were jealous of Sarie because she was as pretty as a princess.

At home Sarie was called the late lamb because she had been born long
after her older brothers.

Her family all worked long, hard hours on the sheep farm, except on
Sundays, when they rested. After lunch her father took a nap, while her
mother sat in the shade of the blue gum tree doing her big, loopy knitting.
But after a few rows she, too, would fall asleep.

Then Sarie would run across the veld to the ridge. That was where Auntie Anna lived. And there she would be, sitting in her rusted-up old car, waiting for Sarie. Then Sarie would climb into the driver's seat and pretend to be taking a Sunday drive somewhere—far, far away.

As they drove, Auntie Anna would tell stories of once upon a time, when she was young and her car was shiny. Then Sarie would tell Auntie Anna everything: how she hated reading aloud, how the words stuck in her throat like dry bread, and how the children laughed at her.

"People can be cruel," said Auntie Anna. "But don't give up, Sarie. It's so good to be able to read well and enjoy books."

One Sunday, tired of driving, Sarie climbed into the back. Dreamily
she ran her hands over the brittle leather, into the darkness between
the seat and the backrest. Then she felt it—something under the seat.
She pulled . . . and out came a dusty old book!

Sarie jumped into the front seat with the book. The cover creaked
as she opened it.

"My goodness, Sarie!" said Auntie Anna. "Look, it says '*To Lizzie with love from Mama and Papa*.' This book belonged to my daughter."

"Read it to me, read it to me!" pleaded Sarie.

The old woman shook her head. "No, Sarie!"

Sarie looked puzzled. Then Auntie Anna's mouth crinkled into a smile. "We will read it together."

"*Once upon a time the wife of a rich man fell ill . . .*"

It was a lovely story about a beautiful girl and her two ugly stepsisters. Reading with Auntie Anna was fun. In some parts Sarie read alone. Then, just before a word could trip her up, Auntie Anna would join in, until the story ended:

"*So Cinderella married her prince and lived happily ever after.*"

As the sun dipped behind the ridge, Auntie Anna closed
the book. Sarie felt too happy to speak.

"It's your book now," said Auntie Anna, patting Sarie's hand.
"Next Sunday we will read it again."

The next day Sarie couldn't wait to get to school. She wanted to show Mr. Adonis her beautiful book.

"Ah, *Cinderella*," said Mr. Adonis.

"Read it to us, sir!" cried the children.

As Mr. Adonis read, Sarie remembered all of it. She could even see some of the words.

Then Mr. Adonis asked the children to take out their reading books. Excitedly, Sarie opened her reading book. But when it was her turn to read aloud, the words tangled around her tongue and she started to stammer.

"Take your time, Sarie," said Mr. Adonis.

Emile looked at Sarie. Her eyes filled with tears as she struggled to get the words out. Charmaine and Carmen giggled behind her.

When Sarie saw Auntie Anna, she told her all about it.
"Emile is the only one who doesn't laugh," said Sarie.
"Well, he sounds like a prince," said Auntie Anna. Then she clapped her hands and said, "And guess who you can be?"

She dashed into her house and came out carrying an old evening dress.
It smelled musty, but it sparkled as it fell over Sarie's shoulders.
"My princess!" declared Auntie Anna with a low bow.

On the Sundays that followed, Sarie read her favorite book for Auntie Anna. The more she read, the less afraid she felt about reading in class. And the less afraid she felt, the better she read.

One day Miss November, the school principal, visited the classroom to hear the children read. One by one they read aloud.

Soon it was Sarie's turn. She opened her reading book, and suddenly the old sick feeling came back. What if she made a mistake and lost her place? What if she found her place, but lost her voice?

Mr. Adonis waited patiently. The class started to fidget. Sarie thought about all the words she had read with Auntie Anna. She could see them—lots of friendly letters holding hands to form words that danced and sang together. She could feel Auntie Anna beside her. Bravely, she took a deep breath and started to read . . .

The words poured out as clear as spring water.

"You read beautifully," said Miss November.

Out of the corner of her eye, Sarie could see Emile smiling.

After school Sarie and Emile walked home together.
"Would you like to go for a drive in my car?" asked Sarie.
Emile laughed. "Where's your car?"
"I'll show you," said Sarie, taking his hand.

When Auntie Anna saw them coming over the hill, she waved.

"Come on! Let's get going!" she shouted. Sarie jumped into the driver's seat. Auntie Anna took the backseat so that Emile could sit in the front.

"So you're Emile," said Auntie Anna.

"Yes," said Emile shyly. "I'm Sarie's friend."

"That's good," said Auntie Anna. "Don't you think she reads beautifully?"

"Yes," said Emile.

"I bet you didn't know she could drive."

"No." Emile giggled.

"Where are we heading to, Sarie?" asked Auntie Anna, settling back.
"Far, far away!" said Sarie.

Before them, the flat expanse of the Little Karoo stretched as far as the
eye could see. Ridges shimmered on the hazy horizon like faraway castles.
And as Sarie took the wheel, the air stood still and it seemed almost . . .

. . . Once Upon a Time.

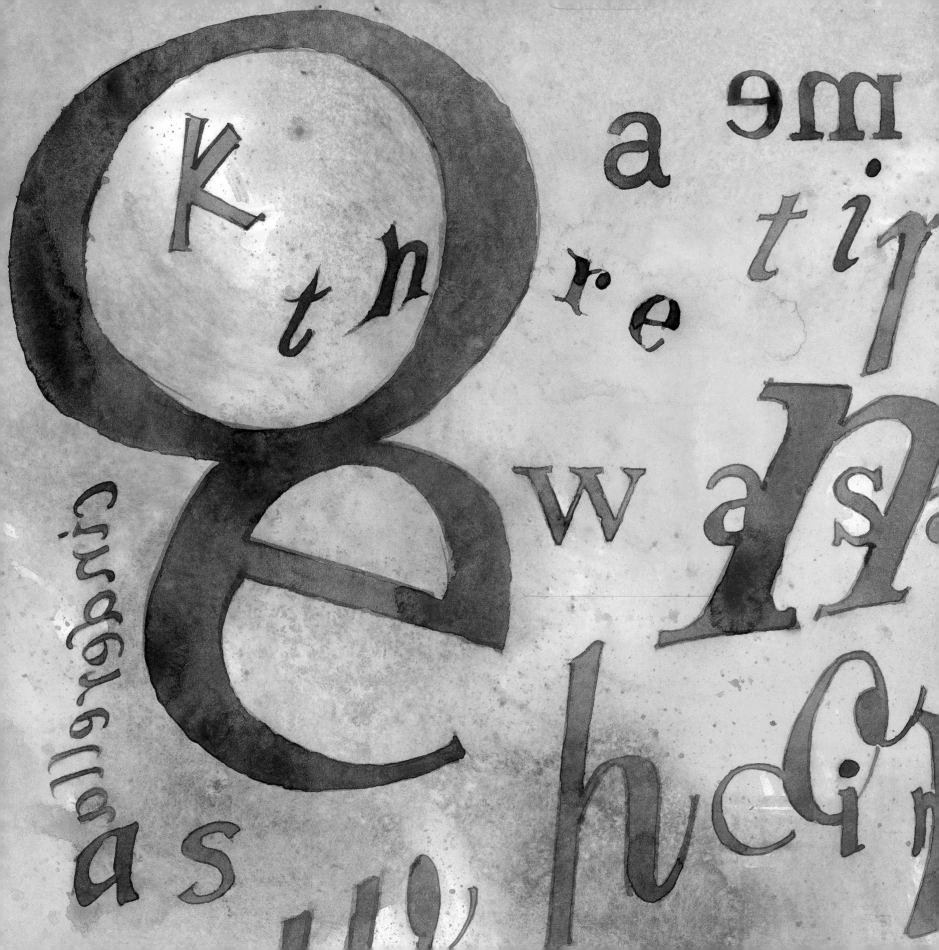